CHILDREN OF THE SUN

CHILDREN OF THE SUN

by
Jan Carew

Illustrated by
Leo and Diane Dillon

Little, Brown and Company
BOSTON   TORONTO

Also written by Jan Carew
and illustrated by Leo and Diane Dillon

THE THIRD GIFT

ILLUSTRATIONS COPYRIGHT © 1980 BY LEO AND DIANE DILLON

TEXT COPYRIGHT © 1976 BY JAN CAREW

FIRST EDITION

Library of Congress Cataloging in Publication Data

Carew, Jan.
  The children of the sun.

  SUMMARY: The Sun asks his two children whether they would rather be great or good. Each son follows a different path.
  [1. Sun--Fiction] I. Dillon, Leo. II. Dillon, Diane. III. Title.
PZ7. C2119Ch   [Fic]   76-8413
ISBN 0-316-12848-1

H

Published simultaneously in Canada
by Little, Brown & Company (Canada) Limited

PRINTED IN THE UNITED STATES OF AMERICA

CHILDREN OF THE SUN

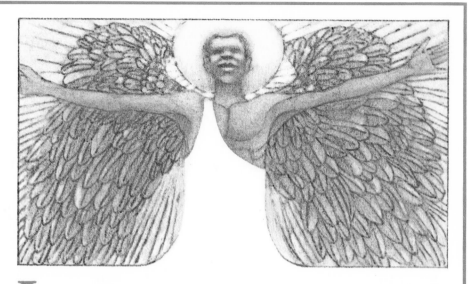

IN LONG TIME PAST DAYS when the Sun was young, the Great Spirit gave him wings. Free as the eagles and red herons, Sun soared along the rim of blue horizons and dodged in and out of the rafters that held up the sky. Sun was young and free, but he was reckless and wild. Sometimes when Wind passed by wearing a cape woven out of mists and rainbows, Sun playfully burnt the edges of the cape, and soon Wind was left naked and angry. Sun plunged into rivers, raising clouds of steam; he danced until his burning feet set the forests ablaze, and often he would trick the stars by telling them how beautiful they were. When they gathered to gaze at their images in still water, he would catch them in a net and scatter them like fireflies across the dark savannahs. Sun spent all his time making merry, and when weariness finally caught up with him, he lay down anywhere that sleep surprised him.

While Sun slept, long spells of darkness filled the skies. The corn never ripened, potatoes rotted in the cold earth, and there were no singing birds at day-clean. The people of the world and their elders were much distressed, so they went to the Great Spirit and complained.

The Great Spirit sat on his gigantic royal stone stool, which was cushioned with moss and striped with a host of rainbow orchids. When he heard the complaints of the people, he said in a voice that moaned like the wind in the wild pine trees: "I will talk to Sun."

As soon as the people and their elders had left, the Great Spirit sent Gé, the condor-bird, to fetch Sun. After searching for many days, Gé found Sun sleeping on a high mountain, cradled in a blanket of snow. With every breath, Sun melted the snow and sent a river cascading down the mountainside.

"Sun," Gé croaked. "Sun," he repeated.

"Leave me alone. Can't you see that I am weary?"

"Sun, I would let you sleep on, but the Great Spirit sent me to you. He says you must come at once."

"Ahhhhh! Mmmmmmmm!" Sun complained, but he arose, banished the lingering webs of sleep by rubbing his body briskly with snow and then flew in silence with Gé to the mountains of Akarai, where the Great Spirit held court.

The Great Spirit was angry and he thundered, "Sun, you must mend your ways. From now on you will no longer have wings and you will no longer spend your time in foolish ways."

"I swear I'll mend my ways, but I beg you, let me keep my wings, Great Spirit," Sun pleaded.

"No! I have decided. Go well, Sun!" the Great Spirit said, and Gé led a contrite Sun away from the heights of Akarai.

For a long time afterward, the wingless sun marked each day by rising and setting monotonously, and each night he rested in the cool, secret caverns under the sea.

But one afternoon when the white cranes and raucous parrots were flying home to their nests, Sun saw a woman, beautiful as the mystery of sleep, lying on the banks of the Potaro River. Her skin had the velvet sheen of the petals of the black narcissus, and her limbs, stretched out carelessly on the white sand, looked as if they were made from streams of dark water. Sun felt his heart jump.

"Dark lady of the white sands of Potaro, what is your name?" he called haltingly.

"Tihona, Ti-ho-na," the mischievous parrots called out. Sun was bewitched by the sleeping woman's beauty and, without thinking twice, he left his familiar path in the sky to come closer. He bent over her, and the sweat from his brow fell into her black hair and became the brightest of jewels.

"Tihona, Ti-ho-na!" chorused the parrots, toucans, and macaws so loudly that the woman woke up. She was frightened and tried to flee, but Sun reached out and held her. Terrified by the touch of his hot hands and the furnace heat of his body, Tihona swooned and fell.

After Sun returned to his place in the sky, Tihona lay quietly among the jewels and pieces of gold he had left strewn across the beach like fallen stars. Only the slightest movement of her breast showed that she was alive.

When morning came, the Great Spirit, who had seen all of Sun's actions, again grew angry and decreed that for as long as the grass grows and the river flows Sun would always remain on his path in the sky.

For her part, Tihona found that she was to give birth to twins. Angered, she went in search of Sun. She crossed mountains and valleys, lakes and savannahs, until she came to the western seashore, and there she waited till Sun was setting. She called out to him: "Sun, I am going to give these twins I am carrying inside me to the sea."

"I am already paying in suffering for what I have done, so spare the twins, Tihona," Sun pleaded. And he fell like a stone beyond the horizon.

The stars and fireflies brightened the night skies, and brooding in the starlight, Tihona could see the silver surf plaiting garlands of foam around the dark rocks. Suddenly voices broke her reverie.

"Mama, don't give us to the cruel sea!" It was the twins inside her who had spoken.

"I must be carrying devils inside me!" Tihona cried.

"Mama, we are your sons, the Children of the Sun. Mama, your heart beats so fiercely that it frightens us."

Tihona sat down in the sand and sighed. The words of the babes had touched her heart. "Hush, go to sleep," she said gently, and they fell asleep knowing that she had accepted them as her sons.

The morning after the twins were born, Gé took Tihona and her sons to the top of Roraima, the red mountain, and the Great Spirit named the boys Pia and Makunaima, the Children of the Sun.

Time passed on the red mountain, and the twins were no longer infants. Tihona loved both her sons equally, but she saw that Makunaima was a rebellious, haughty child, and wild fires burned in the depths of his eyes. Pia, the gentle one, was often beaten by his wild brother, but he did not complain.

Then, one morning bright with dew and singing birds, Gé appeared and announced to Tihona: "The Great Spirit says I must take the Children of the Sun to him."

Tihona, full of fear and sorrow, said: "Gé, I beg of you, tell the Great Spirit that my sons are still young saplings that any wind can break. In a few years they will be strong enough to resist a hurricane. Then they can do the Spirit's bidding. Plead with him for me, Gé."

"The Great Spirit says the Children of the Sun must visit him now."

"But why is he harassing us like this, Gé?" Tihona asked.

"Don't ask me. I'm only the messenger," Gé grumbled.

The twins sat on Gé's back, and after flying for a long time, he finally brought them to the heights of Akarai.

The Great Spirit welcomed them and bade them sit beside him on the mossy cushions of his great stone stool.

"Would you like to be good men or great men?" the Great Spirit asked after they were seated. When neither Pia nor Makunaima replied at once, he frowned and said: "Then you must both travel to the ends of the earth in search of an answer to this question."

So through endless seasons the brothers traveled to the four corners of the world. They sailed down Rivers of Night with vampires piloting their canoe, crossed seas and deserts, forests and plains, but neither could choose for himself an answer to the Great Spirit's question. Finally, worn out by their endless journeyings, they came to a mountain pool.

On the opposite side of the pool was Wa-uno, the White Crane, who was part magician and part bird. While they sat resting, they saw Wa-uno strike his beak against a flint and send off sparks.

"Do that again, Crane," the twins begged. Crane struck the flint again and again, and each time sparks flew in all directions. The Children of the Sun caught the sparks and soon learned the art of making fire. The twins then thanked Crane for leading them to the gift of fire and set forth again on their quest.

As they traveled, Makunaima kept the wonderful secret of making fire to himself, thinking that someday it would give him power, but Pia shared it with all the people of the world. It warmed the bones of those who shivered through cold nights and kept roaming brute-beasts from the haunts of men.

After many years of wandering, Pia and Maku-maima returned to their mother. The wait for her sons had streaked Tihona's hair with gray, and her face, beating against so many anxious years, was lined by time and suffering. At first Tihona could not believe that her sons had returned, and she often woke up in the middle of the night to gaze at them while they slept. One night when she was bending over Makunaima, her hair brushed against his eyes. Half asleep, he sprang up, thinking that a beast of prey was upon him. Frightened, Tihona ran away into the night, but her son jumped out of his hammock and followed her. Still dazed by sleep, he did not realize that it was his mother, and he seized her around the waist. She cried out, waking Pia from a dreamless sleep. He saw a shadowy figure wrestling with his mother, and reached for his spear. Tihona's warning shout reached Pia too late, and he plunged the spear into his brother's heart. Makunaima was dead, yet not a drop of blood stained the innocent grass on which he lay. And on the dark savannah snakes formed a circle around his corpse to hiss a devil's requiem all night.

Pia, grieving because he had killed his brother, kept a vigil with his mother beyond the circle of snakes and waited for day-clean. As soon as Father Sun appeared, Pia shot arrows into the air. Weaving them with sunlight, he made a ladder, said good-bye to his mother, and climbed until he came to the house of his father.

He found Father Sun lying in his hammock in an immense circle of light. Sun looked at Pia with burning anthracite eyes, and with a hand that sprouted tongues of flame offered him a hammock next to his. Pia now told how he had killed his twin by accident, and Father Sun, touched by the despair in his son's voice, said, "Pia, you must return to the earth and bring Makunaima's body to my house before I end my journey to the Western Caves."

Pia made the journey to and from the earth with the speed of a deer, and very gently he placed Makunaima's body in the center of the largest room of Father Sun's house. Father Sun melted the spear that had pierced Makunaima's heart and brought him back to life. Pia rejoiced to see his brother live again.

The twins now stayed with their father. There were three suns in the sky, and the people of the earth had three shadows. But the rebellious Makunaima would not follow the trail that Father Sun had marked out for him across the heavens. For he had finally decided in his heart to be a great man, and he believed that the great have no use for rules. Father Sun scolded him and Pia pleaded with him, but this only incited Makunaima to more lawless actions.

One afternoon, deciding to visit his mother's house, he journeyed to the earth. The next day the people of the Human World complained to Father Sun that Makunaima had turned their rivers and lakes into boiling cauldrons, and the forests into a million torches in the wind. After hearing the people's complaints, Father Sun summoned his sons to the brightest room in his house. When they entered, he said sternly: "You must make recompense to the Earth People."

"I will make recompense, Father Sun," Pia said, but Makunaima laughed and shouted: "I was only trying to visit my mother's house. Why are you, of all people, scolding me, Father Sun? You have behaved in the same way. And have you ever done anything for our mother, Tihona, except cause her grief?"

"I should have left you to the vultures," Sun bellowed. Then Makunaima grew angry and struck his father in the face. Father Sun wept tears of anger and, in a terrible rage, seized his son around the waist. Flames from the old man's heart turned Makunaima into cinders and ashes, and he was scattered by the wind.

Having destroyed the thankless Makunaima, Father Sun ordered Pia to stay with him and continue the endless journeys back and forth across the heavens. Now there were two suns in the sky. But Pia, longing to see his mother again, pleaded with Father Sun:

"Let me go back and complete my mission in the Human World, for at last I know that I want to be a good man and bring peace and harmony to all. When my task is done I will return and stay with you forever."

Father Sun knew that his child's task might never be finished, but he allowed Pia to return to earth. When he arrived, Pia took Tihona to the top of Roraima and built a home for her on the very spot where he and Makunaima had lived as children. She lives there to this day, waiting for Pia to finish his endless task. Weaving curtains of mist and rainbows around her, she weeps for her lost sons. Her tears run down the cliff-face of the mountain, flowing into rills, brooks and rivers, and the sea carries them to the shores of the whole world.